D1399953

THE TURNIP

AN OLD RUSSIAN FOLKTALE ILLUSTRATED BY

PIERR MORGAN

The Putnam & Grosset Group

Printed on recycled paper

There are many versions of this old Russian tale;
this one, collected from a Russian storyteller by
Katherine Milhous and Alice Dalgliesh for
ONCE ON A TIME (Charles Scribner's Sons, 1938)
is particularly popular with storytellers because
of the rhythm and happy repetition of sounds.

Text reprinted by arrangement with Charles Scribner's Sons,
an imprint of Macmillan Publishing Company,
from ONCE ON A TIME, copyright 1938 by Charles Scribner's Sons.
Illustrations copyright © 1990 by Pierr Morgan.
A PaperStar Book, published in 1996 by The Putnam & Grosset Group,
200 Madison Avenue, New York, NY 10016.
PaperStar Books and the PaperStar logo are trademarks of
The Putnam Berkley Group, Inc. Originally published in 1990 by
Philomel Books. Published simultaneously in Canada.
Printed in the United States of America.
Library of Congress Cataloging-in-Publication Data
Morgan, Pierr.   The turnip/illustrated by Pierr Morgan.   p.   cm.
Summary: One of Dedoushka's turnips grows to such an enormous size that
the whole family, including the dog, cat, and mouse, is needed to pull it up.
[1. Folklore—Soviet Union.]   I. Title.   PZ8.1.M824Tu
1990   398.2'1'0947—dc20   89-34023   CIP   AC
ISBN 0-698-11426-4
10   9   8   7   6   5   4   3   2   1

For Art and Ruthie
and most especially Aaron Morgan Leitz.
I love you to pieces.

One warm spring day
Dedoushka planted
a turnip seed.
This turnip grew

and grew

and became very, very

...large.

Then Dedoushka walked to the field
and tried to pull the turnip.
He pulled,
      and pulled
            and pulled.

"Oh! Oh! Oh! I cannot pull the turnip,"
Dedoushka said.

"Baboushka, dear," he called to his wife, "please come and help me, I cannot pull the turnip."

"You are old and weak, Dedoushka. I will help you pull the turnip."

Dedoushka and Baboushka walked to the field.
Dedoushka pulled at the turnip.
Baboushka pulled at Dedoushka.
And they pulled
            and pulled
                    and pulled.

"Uh, uh, uh, we cannot pull the turnip,"
said Baboushka. "I will call Mashenka,
she is young and strong. She will help us
pull the turnip."

"Mashenka, Mashenka," she called to her granddaughter.

"Here I am! Here I am! What is it, Baboushka?"
"Please come and help us pull the turnip."
"Surely I will. That is easy, Baboushka."

Dedoushka pulled at the turnip,
Baboushka pulled at Dedoushka,
Mashenka pulled at Baboushka
and they pulled
              and pulled
                      and pulled.

"Ah, ah, ah," said Mashenka, "we cannot
pull the turnip. We will call Geouchka.
He is a good dog and he will help us."

"Geouchka! Geouchka! Come and help us."

"Bow, wow, wow," barked Geouchka
as he ran to the field.

Dedoushka pulled at the turnip,
Baboushka pulled at Dedoushka,
Mashenka pulled at Baboushka,
Geouchka pulled at Mashenka
and they pulled
                    and pulled
                              and pulled.

"Bow, wow, wow, we cannot
pull the turnip," barked Geouchka.
"We will call Keska. She is a very
clever cat and she will help us."

"Kes-kess, come and help us," called Geouchka. "We cannot pull the turnip."

"Meou, meou, meou, I don't eat turnips but I will help you! Meou, meou, meou!"

Dedoushka pulled at the turnip,
Baboushka pulled at Dedoushka,
Mashenka pulled at Baboushka,
Geouchka pulled at Mashenka,
Keska pulled at Geouchka
and they pulled
              and pulled
                      and pulled.

"Meou, meou, we cannot
pull the turnip," cried Keska.
"I will call the little field mouse.
She will help us."

"The little field mouse?" the others said.

"Yes," and Keska cried,
"Little field mouse, little field mouse!
Come and help us. We cannot pull the turnip."

"Ee, ee, ee," squeaked the little field mouse.
"I will help you pull the turnip."

Dedoushka pulled
at the turnip,
Baboushka pulled
at Dedoushka,
Mashenka pulled
at Baboushka,
Geouchka pulled
at Mashenka,
Keska pulled
at Geouchka,
the little field
mouse pulled
at Keska.

And out came the turnip!